Arthur's teacher, Mr. Ratburn, explained homework.

"What should the story be about?" Arthur

"Anything," Mr. Ratburn said. "Write about something that is important to you."

Arthur started his story the minute he got home.
He knew exactly what he wanted to write about.

How I Got My Puppy Pal

I always wanted a dog, but first I had to prove I was responsible. So I started Arthur's Pet Business. My mom made me keep all the animals in the basement. It was a lot of work, but it was fun until I thought I lost Perky. But then I found her, and she had three puppies! And I got to keep one of them. That's how I got my dog Pal.

The End

Arthur read his story to D.W.

"That's a boring story," D.W. said. "Does it have to be real life? Because your life is so dull."

"I don't want to write a boring story," said Arthur.

"If it were me," D.W. suggested, "I'd make the story about getting an elephant."

The next day, Arthur read his new story to Buster.

"Did you like the part about the elephant puppies?" he asked.

"It's okay, I guess," said Buster. "I'm writing a cool story about outer space."

Maybe my story should take place on the moon, thought Arthur.

On Wednesday, Arthur read his newest story to the Brain.

"Scientifically speaking, elephants would weigh less on the moon, but wouldn't float that high," said the Brain.

"So you don't like it?" asked Arthur.

"A good story should be well researched," said the Brain. "Like mine: 'If I Had a Pet Stegosaurus in the Jurassic Period.'"

Arthur hurried to the library.

"What are all those books for?" asked Francine.

"Research," said Arthur. "I'm writing about my pet five-toed mammal of the genus *Loxodonta*."

"Your *what?*" asked Francine.

"My elephant!" Arthur explained.

"Oh," said Francine. "I'm putting jokes in my story."

All through dinner, Arthur worried about his story.
"Please pass the corn," asked Father.

"Corn! That's it!" said Arthur. "Purple corn and blue elephants! On Planet Shmellafint! Now *that's* funny."

"Arthur is acting weirder than usual," said D.W.

On Thursday, everyone at the Sugar Bowl was talking about their stories.

"Last year, a kid wrote a country-western song for her story," said Prunella. "And she got an A+."

"How do you know?" asked Arthur.

"That kid was me," explained Prunella. "Mr. Ratburn said I should send it to a record company. It was *that* good."

"Wow!" said Arthur.

That night, Arthur's imagination went wild. He decided to turn his story into a song. He even made up a dance to go with it.

Later, he tried it out on his family.
"...Now this little boy
Can go home and enjoy
His own personal striped elephant.
And you will see
How happy he will be
Here on Planet...Shmellafint!"

"Well," said Arthur. "What do you think?"

Mother and Father smiled.
"It's nice," said Grandma Thora. "But a little confusing."
"Too bad you can't dance," said D.W.

"What am I going to do?" said Arthur. "My story
is due tomorrow."
That night Arthur didn't sleep very well.

The next day, Arthur worried until Mr. Ratburn finally called on him.

When Arthur's song and dance was over, the classroom was so quiet, it was almost spooky. Binky raised his hand. "Did that really happen?"

"Sort of," said Arthur. "It started as the story of how I got my dog."

"I'd like to hear that story," said Mr. Ratburn.

"The title was 'How I Got My Puppy Pal,'" said Arthur.

Arthur told how proud he was of his pet business and how scared he was when Perky disappeared. And he told how happy he was to find her under his bed and how surprised he was to see her three puppies.

"And the best part is," said Arthur, "I got to keep one!"

Buster said, "I like that story better than your other one."

"Great story!" said Binky.

"I think Arthur's story was the best!" said Francine.

"Good work," said Mr. Ratburn. "Of course, I expect you to write it all down by Monday."

Then Mr. Ratburn gave Arthur a gold sticker. "Oh, and one more thing," he said.

"Leave out the dancing!"